And when the birds wake up in the morning in Miseryland, they don't start singing.

They start crying!

Oh, it really is an awful place!

little Miss Sunshine

by Roger Hargreaves

WORLD INTERNATIONAL
MANCHESTER

Welcome to Miseryland.

We say 'welcome', but there really isn't very much to welcome you about it.

It's the most miserable place in the world.

Miseryland worms look like this!

And the King of Miseryland is even worse.

He sits on his throne all day long with tears streaming down his face.

"Oh I'm so unhappy," he keeps sobbing, over and over and over again.

Dear, oh dear, oh dear!

Little Miss Sunshine had been on holiday.

She'd had a lovely time, and now she was driving home.

She was whistling happily to herself as she drove along when, out of the corner of her eye, she saw a signpost.

To Miseryland.

"Miseryland?" she thought to herself.

"I've never heard of that before!"

And she turned off down the road.

She came to a sign which read:

YOU ARE NOW ENTERING MISERYLAND

And underneath it said:

SMILING

LAUGHING

CHUCKLING

GIGGLING

FORBIDDEN

By Order of the King.

"Oh dear," thought little Miss Sunshine as she drove along.

She came to a castle with a huge door.

A soldier stopped her.

"What do you want?" he asked gloomily.

"I want to see the King," smiled little Miss Sunshine.

"You're under arrest," said the soldier.

"But why?" asked little Miss Sunshine.

"For a most serious crime," replied the soldier.

"Most serious indeed!"

The soldier marched little Miss Sunshine through the huge door.

And across a courtyard.

And through another huge door.

And up an enormous staircase.

And along a long corridor.

And through another huge door.

And into a gigantic room.

And at the end of the gigantic room sat the King.

Crying his eyes out!

"Your Majesty," said the soldier, bowing low, "I have arrested this person for a most serious crime!"

The King stopped crying.

"She smiled at me," said the soldier.

There was a shocked silence.

"She did WHAT?" cried the King.

"She smiled at me," repeated the soldier.

"But why is smiling not allowed?" laughed little Miss Sunshine.

"She LAUGHED at me," cried the King.

"Why not?" she chuckled.

"She CHUCKLED!" cried the King.

Little Miss Sunshine giggled.

"She GIGGLED!" went on the King.

And he burst into tears again.

"But why are these things not allowed?"
asked little Miss Sunshine.

"Because this is Miseryland," wept the King.

"And they've never been allowed," he sobbed.

"Oh, I was so unhappy before you arrived,"
he wailed, "but now I'm twice as unhappy!"

Little Miss Sunshine looked at him.

"But wouldn't you like to be happy?"
she asked.

"Of course I would," cried the King.

"But how can I be? This is MISERYLAND!"

Little Miss Sunshine thought.

"Come on," she said.

"You can't talk to me like that," sobbed
the King.

"Don't be silly," she replied, and led him across
the gigantic room, and through the huge door,
and along the long corridor, and down the
enormous staircase, and through the huge
door, and across the courtyard, and through
the huge door, to her car.

"Get in," she said.

Little Miss Sunshine drove the crying King back to the large notice.

"Dry your eyes," she said, and handed him a large handkerchief from her handbag.

And then, from her handbag, she produced a large pen.

Five minutes later she'd finished.

Instead of saying:

YOU ARE NOW ENTERING MISERYLAND
    SMILING
    LAUGHING
    CHUCKLING
    GIGGLING
    FORBIDDEN
    By Order of the King.

Do you know what it said now?

YOU ARE NOW ENTERING LAUGHTERLAND
    SMILING
    LAUGHING
    CHUCKLING
    GIGGLING
    PERMITTED
    By Order of the King

"There," said little Miss Sunshine. "Now you can be happy."

"But I don't know HOW to be happy," sniffed the King.

"I've never TRIED it!"

"Nonsense," said little Miss Sunshine.

"It's really very easy," she smiled.

The King tried a smile.

"Not bad," she laughed.

The King tried a laugh.

"Getting better," she chuckled.

The King tried a chuckle.

"You've got it," she giggled.

The King looked at her.

"So I have," he giggled.

"I'm the King of Laughterland!"

As little Miss Sunshine arrived home, there was Mr Happy out for an evening stroll.

"Hello," he grinned. "Where have you been?"

"Miseryland!" she replied.

"Miseryland?" he said.

"I didn't know there was such a place!"

Little Miss Sunshine giggled.

"Actually," she said.

"There isn't!"

SPECIAL OFFERS FOR MR MEN AND LITTLE MISS READERS

In every Mr Men and Little Miss book you will find a special token. Collect only six tokens and we will send you a super poster of your choice featuring all your favourite Mr Men or Little Miss friends.

And for the first 4,000 readers we hear from, we will send you a Mr Men activity pad* and a bookmark* as well – absolutely free!

Return this page with six tokens from Mr Men and/or Little Miss books to:
Marketing Department, World International Publishing, Egmont House,
PO Box 111, 61 Great Ducie Street, Manchester M60 3BL.

Your name:_____

Address:_____

_____

_____ Postcode: _____

Signature of parent or guardian: _____

I enclose **six** tokens – please send me a Mr Men poster ☐

I enclose **six** tokens – please send me a Little Miss poster ☐

We may occasionally wish to advise you of other children's books that we publish. If you would rather we didn't, please tick this box ☐

*while stocks last (Please note: this offer is limited to a maximum of two posters per household.)

Collect six of these tokens. You will find one inside every Mr Men and Little Miss book which has this special offer.

1 TOKEN

MR MEN question time – can you help?

Thank you for purchasing this Mr Men or Little Miss pocket book. We would be most grateful if you would help us with the answers to a few questions.

Would you be interested in a presentation box
to keep your Mr Men or Little Miss books in?   **Yes** ☐ **No** ☐ (please tick)

Apart from Mr Men or Little Miss, who
is your favourite children's character? _____

If you could write a Mr Men and a Little Miss book,
what names would you give your characters?   **Mr** _____

Little Miss _____

If applicable, where did you buy this book from?
Please give the stockist's name and address.

Name: _____

Address: _____

_____

_____

THANK YOU FOR YOUR HELP